MEG & MOG

3 Terrific Tales

by Helen Nicoll
and Jan Pieńkowski

PUFFIN BOOKS

for Sam

MEG'S VEG

by Helen Nicoll
and Jan Pieńkowski

PUFFIN BOOKS

It was springtime. Time for Meg
to start her vegetable garden

Meg fetched the muck

Owl
sowed
peas
and
carrots

Mog
put in
a
pumpkin

Meg
sowed
some
seeds
she
had
found
in
her
cauldron

It was so cold, no seeds grew

Mog
made
a
scarecrow
to
guard
his
pumpkin

BRRRR

Meg tried to make the sun shine

Make a sunshine spell

The
sun shone.

It got
hotter

and
hotter

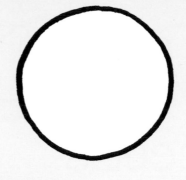

and
hotter

The rain came down in sheets

They had

They
made
a
huge
compost
heap

Then
they
had to
stake
the
peas

They had to hoe down the rows

and water the pumpkin

And then,
they
had to
eat
them
all

Goodbye!

for Emms

MOG at the ZOO

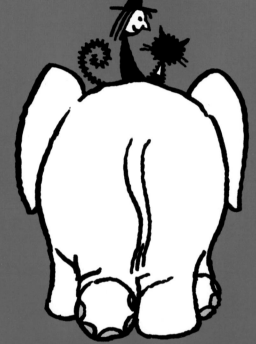

by Helen Nicoll
and Jan Pieńkowski

PUFFIN BOOKS

Meg, Mog and Owl went to the zoo

The keepers looked at Mog

He flew past the flamingos

He zipped past the zebras

The crocodiles gave him a cheer

GO! GO! GO!

and
ran
slap
into
a tree

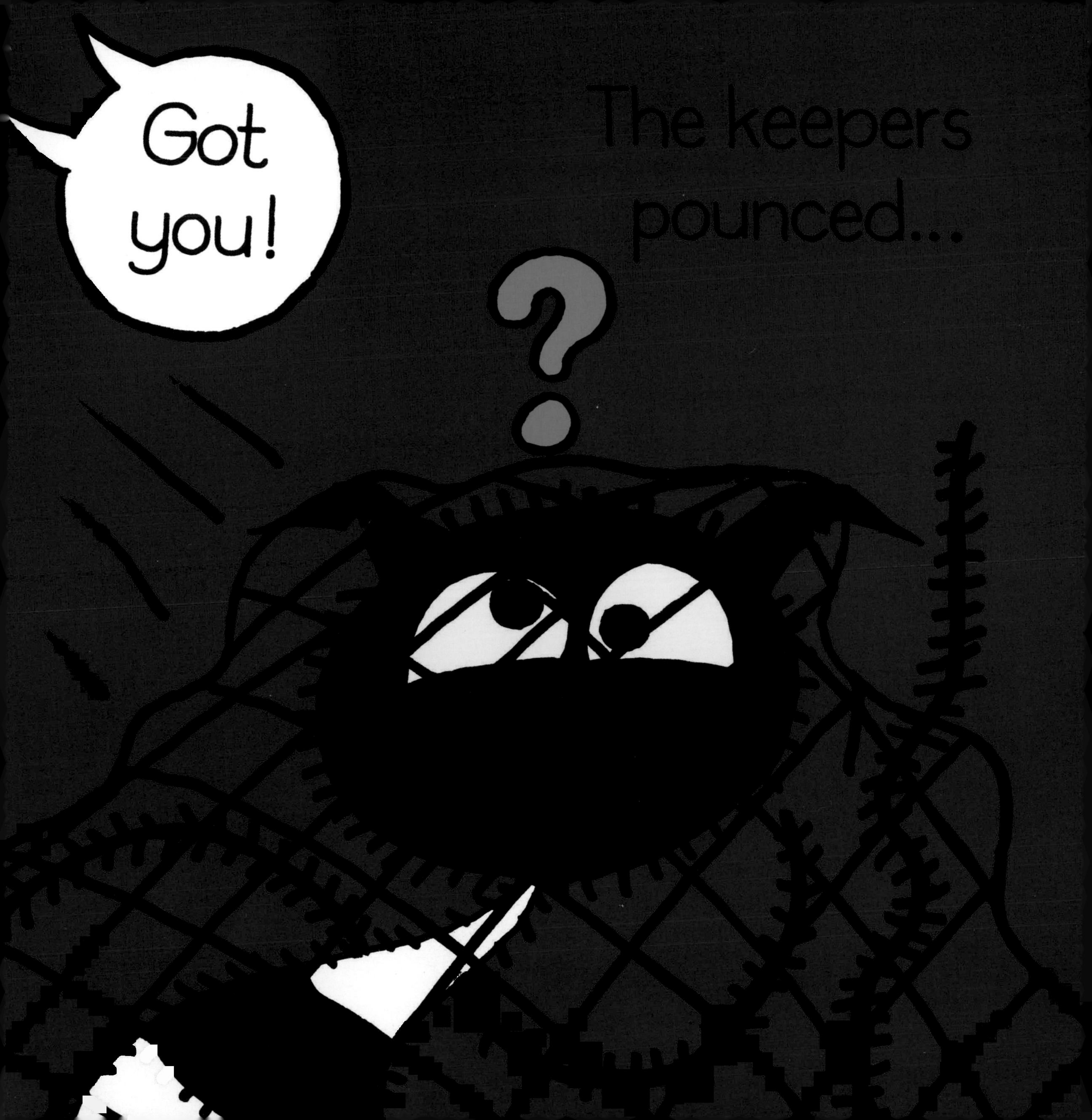

The keepers pounced...

They put Mog in a cage and went

away to look him up in a book

An elephant gave her a bun

Pandemonium broke out

CHATTER

SQUAWK

ROAR

HOWL

MONK

..Squeak

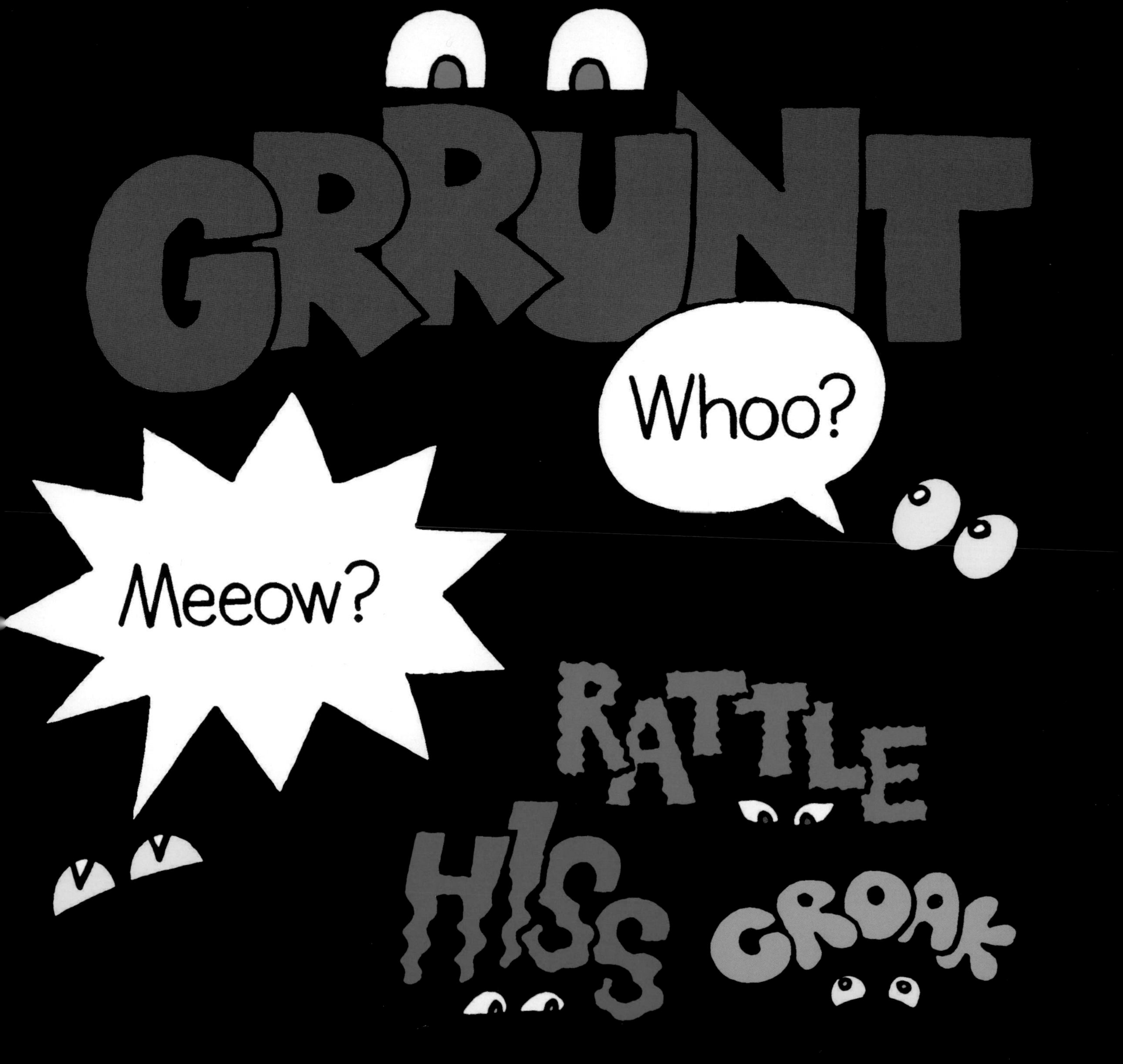
GRRUNT
Whoo?
Meeow?
RATTLE
HISS
CROAK

They had
breakfast
in a
tree

Goodbye!

for Abigail

MEG up the CREEK

by Helen Nicoll
and Jan Pieńkowski
PUFFIN BOOKS

and into the wood

Owl went to find Meg

Have a blackberry...

They rushed back

Meg put in

7 snails

4 fire flies

a bird's nest

and a snap dragon

The fire lit

Goodbye!